Karen's Big Job

**Other books by
Ann M. Martin**

Leo the Magnificat
Rachel Parker, Kindergarten Show-off
Eleven Kids, One Summer
Ma and Pa Dracula
Yours Turly, Shirley
Ten Kids, No Pets
With You and Without You
Me and Katie (the Pest)
Stage Fright
Inside Out
Bummer Summer

For older readers:
Missing Since Monday
Just a Summer Romance
Slam Book

THE BABY-SITTERS CLUB series
THE BABY-SITTERS CLUB mysteries
THE KIDS IN MS. COLMAN'S CLASS series
BABY-SITTERS LITTLE SISTER series
(see inside book covers for a complete listing)

Little Sister

Karen's Big Job
Ann M. Martin

Illustrations by Susan Tang

A
LITTLE APPLE
PAPERBACK

SCHOLASTIC INC.
New York Toronto London Auckland Sydney

The author gratefully acknowledges
Diane Molleson
for her help
with this book.

ISBN 0-590-69192-9

12 11 10 9 8 7 6 5 4 3 2 1   7 8 9/9 0 1 2/0

Printed in the U.S.A   40

First Scholastic printing, April 1997

The Lilac Tree

"Karen, where are you?" I heard my little brother Andrew calling. Andrew is four going on five.

"In the backyard," I shouted. (People are always telling me to keep my voice down. But I wanted to be sure Andrew heard me.) I was sitting on a stone bench under the lilac tree. It was the beginning of April, and the lilacs were starting to bloom. I adore lilacs and roses and daffodils. But especially lilacs.

I am Karen Brewer. I am seven years old. I have long blonde hair, blue eyes, and some

freckles. (I have more freckles in the summer.) I also wear glasses. I even have two pairs. The blue pair is for reading. The pink pair is for the rest of the time.

"Hi, Karen," Andrew said when he saw me. "I found her!" he called over his shoulder.

"Who are you talking to?" I asked.

"To Kristy," answered Andrew. "She was looking for you, too."

"What for?" I asked. (Kristy is my older stepsister. She is also one of my favorite people ever.)

"You'll see," said Andrew. (I hate it when he does that.)

"Oh, there you are, Karen," said Kristy. "Wait here. I have to go find the others."

The others turned out to be my stepbrothers: David Michael, Sam, and Charlie. Soon all six of us were sitting under the lilac tree.

"I call this family meeting to order," said Kristy.

Kristy is used to being in charge of meetings. She is president of the Baby-sitters

Club. She and her friends meet three times a week to run a baby-sitting business.

"Why are we having this meeting?" I asked.

Kristy gave me a funny look. "Didn't Andrew tell you?"

I shook my head.

Andrew giggled.

"Mom's birthday is at the end of this month," Kristy explained. "I thought we should start thinking about what we could do for her."

"Let's give Elizabeth a big party," I said. I love to plan parties.

Elizabeth is Kristy's mother, my step-mother. I was glad her birthday was this month, so Andrew and I could go to her party. Our parents are divorced. We spend every other month with Daddy and Elizabeth at the big house, where we are now. The rest of the time we live with Mommy and my stepfather, Seth, at the little house.

"I was thinking of a big party too," said Kristy. She pulled out a notebook and wrote

4

down my idea. (Kristy is very organized.)

"What about taking her bowling instead?" asked Sam.

"Mom doesn't like to bowl," said Kristy.

"I know. I was just kidding," said Sam. Sam is a big tease.

"Why don't we take her to a play?" said David Michael. "A Broadway play in New York City." (David Michael loves the theater. He acts in all his school plays and wants to be an actor when he grows up.)

Kristy wrote down "Play in New York City." I could tell the others did not think the play was such a good idea.

"It would cost a lot for all of us to see a Broadway play," said Charlie.

Kristy nodded. "It's true. We should plan something we could do together as a family. Emily Michelle is too young for a play. She would never sit still."

That's for sure, I said to myself. (Emily Michelle is my youngest sister. She is only two and a half.)

"What about a beach party?" asked An-

5

drew. "We could have a picnic by the water and then go swimming."

"It is too cold to swim this time of year," I said.

Kristy nodded. "And it might rain on the day of Mom's birthday. It rains a lot in April."

Everyone had a lot more ideas. Charlie wanted to take Elizabeth to a dog show. Sam wanted to throw her a pizza party. David Michael wanted it to be an ice-cream party. In the end we voted. (That was Kristy's idea.) We decided to give Elizabeth a party at the big house. If it was warm and sunny, we would have the party outside in my favorite place — under the lilac tree.

My Two Houses

"Andrew, have you seen my pink sneakers?" I asked. My voice sounded muffled because I was under my bed looking for them.

"No," answered Andrew.

Darn. I love my pink sneakers. I was getting ready to play outside, and I really wanted to wear them. Not the ratty old red ones I had on. Then I remembered something. I might have left them at the little house. Boo and bullfrogs!

Remember I told you that Andrew and I

live in a big house and a little house? Now I will tell you more about them.

A long time ago, when I was very little, Andrew and I lived with Mommy and Daddy in one house in Stoneybrook, Connecticut. Then Mommy and Daddy started fighting — at first a little, then a lot. Finally they got a divorce. They told us they still loved Andrew and me very much, but they did not love each other anymore. So Mommy moved out of the big house. (It is the house Daddy grew up in.) She moved to a little house, not far away. Then Mommy married Seth. He is my stepfather. Daddy married again too. He married Elizabeth.

Here is who is in my little-house family: Mommy, Seth, Andrew, me, Rocky and Midgie (Seth's cat and dog), Emily Junior (my very own rat), and Bob (Andrew's hermit crab).

Here are the people in my big-house family: Daddy, Elizabeth, Andrew, me, Kristy, Charlie, Sam, David Michael, Emily Michelle, and Nannie. There are also lots of

8

pets in the big house: Shannon, Boo-Boo, Goldfishie, Crystal Light the Second, Emily Junior, and Bob. (Emily Junior and Bob go back and forth when Andrew and I do.)

Kristy, Charlie, Sam, and David Michael are Elizabeth's children. (She was married once before too.) Charlie and Sam are old. They go to high school. David Michael is seven like me. But he is an older seven than I am. Kristy, as I told you, is one of my favorite people ever. She is thirteen, but she still plays with me a lot. Emily Michelle is my adopted sister. I love her very much. (That is why I named my pet rat after her.) Daddy and Elizabeth adopted Emily Michelle from the faraway country of Vietnam. Nannie is Elizabeth's mother. (That makes her my stepgrandmother.) She helps take care of the big house and all us kids. She also helps take care of the pets. Shannon is David Michael's puppy. Boo-Boo is Daddy's fat old cat. And Goldfishie and Crystal Light the Second are goldfish who belong to Andrew and me.

I made up special nicknames for my brother and me. I call us Andrew Two-Two and Karen Two-Two. I thought up those names after my teacher read a book to our class. It was called *Jacob Two-Two Meets the Hooded Fang.* Andrew and I are two-twos because we have two of so many things. We have two houses and two families, two mommies, two daddies, two cats, and two dogs. Plus I have two bicycles, one at each house. (Andrew has two trikes). I have two stuffed cats that look exactly alike. Goosie lives at the little house. Moosie stays at the big house. And we have two sets of clothes, books, and toys. I even have two pieces of Tickly, my special blanket. This way, we do not need to pack much when we go back and forth. (Except once in awhile, I do forget something, such as my pink sneakers.)

I also have a best friend near each house. Hannie Papadakis lives near Daddy's. Nancy Dawes lives next door to Mommy's. Hannie, Nancy, and I are all in Ms. Colman's second-grade class at Stoneybrook Academy. We do everything together.

Being a two-two is not very hard. Sometimes Andrew and I miss the family we are not staying with. But mostly we are lucky. Think how many people love us.

"Karen," Andrew called from downstairs. "Nannie found your pink sneakers. One was in the kitchen. Shannon took the other one to the living room."

"Oh, goody. Thank you, Nannie." I ran downstairs and wrapped my arms around Nannie's waist. I had my pink sneakers. And I had a whole month ahead of me with my big-house family.

An Important Day

"Do I have to eat this cabbage?" asked David Michael.

"Yes," answered Elizabeth. "I thought you liked corned beef and cabbage."

"I like corned beef," David Michael said as he pushed the cabbage to one side of his plate.

My big-house family was sitting at the long dining-room table eating a New England boiled dinner. That is what Nannie called it. And I can see why. Everything was boiled — the corned beef, the cabbage, the

carrots, the potatoes, and the turnips. I thought it was delicious.

"Karen, Kristy," Daddy said as he passed the plate of rolls to Elizabeth. "Did you know that Take Our Daughters To Work Day is coming up soon?"

I put my fork down. "What does that mean?" I asked.

"It means Mommy and Watson can take us to work with them," Kristy explained. (All of Elizabeth's children call Daddy Watson.)

"Me, too?" asked Emily Michelle. She put her plastic milk cup down with a thump.

"No, Emily. You are still a little too young to come to work with us," answered Elizabeth.

Emily pouted.

"Oh, cheer up, Emily," said Sam. "One day you will be older like us. Then you will wish you could stay home and play."

"Are you going to miss school that day?" David Michael wanted to know.

"Yup," answered Kristy as she bit into a roll.

"Wow," said David Michael. His eyes became a little rounder. "This must be a pretty important day."

"It is," said Elizabeth. "It will give Kristy and Karen a chance to see what grown-ups do at work. And that may encourage them to start thinking about what they would like to do when they finish school."

"Oh, I already know what I want to be when I grow up," I said. "I want to be a famous movie star. Or maybe a singer in a rock band."

"So I guess a career in advertising or insurance isn't for you," Sam teased. Elizabeth works for an advertising agency in Stamford. And Daddy works for a big insurance company. He works at home most of the time.

"Well, I guess I could think about it," I said.

Everyone laughed.

"Can boys go to work that day, too?" asked David Michael.

"No," said Elizabeth. "This is a special day just for girls."

"Bummer," said David Michael. "I could use a day off from school."

Daddy cleared his throat. "Now, Karen and Kristy. Elizabeth and I were thinking it would be good for you to see what both of us do. So we thought Karen could go to work with Elizabeth in the morning while Kristy stays here with me. At lunchtime I will drive Kristy to Elizabeth's office and bring Karen home for the afternoon. How does that plan sound?"

"Great," Kristy and I answered at once. I could not wait. April was turning out to be a fun month.

Party Plans

"Let's definitely not have cabbage or carrots at this party," said David Michael.

"Since when do you hate vegetables so much?" asked Kristy.

"Since always," answered David Michael. Kristy rolled her eyes. Kristy, Andrew, David Michael, Sam, Charlie, and I were sitting in Kristy's room planning Elizabeth's birthday party.

"We need a theme for this party," Kristy was saying.

"You mean like a magician or something?" asked David Michael.

"Sort of," answered Kristy. "I was thinking of an idea that could tie the party together." We were all quiet for a moment.

"What about a flower party?" I asked. "We could pick big bunches of lilacs to put on every table. And I could wear my dress with the purple and yellow flowers on it."

"And Charlie and I could wear our flowered Hawaiian shirts," said Sam. The others laughed.

"You know," said Kristy, "having a flower theme is not a bad idea. Mom loves flowers."

"That's true," said Charlie. He leaned back in Kristy's beanbag chair. "What about also making it a surprise party?"

"Do you think we could keep it a secret?" asked Sam.

"If we had to, we could," I said firmly.

"Does that mean we cannot even tell Daddy or Nannie?" asked Andrew.

"No, we can tell them," said Kristy. "We

18

will need them to help us set things up." She was busy writing "Surprise party/flower theme" in her notebook. "But maybe we should not tell Emily Michelle. She will enjoy the surprise as much as Mom will."

I nodded. I knew what else Kristy was thinking — Emily Michelle would not be able to keep the party a secret.

"What about presents?" asked David Michael.

Oops. I had almost forgotten about presents. Luckily the others had not. David Michael wanted to write a skit for Elizabeth and perform it at the party. Kristy was going to sew her a pillow in the shape of a cat. (Her friend Mary Anne was going to help her.) Sam and Charlie decided to make her a footstool. (They were taking woodworking at school.) Andrew wanted to draw her a picture. Everyone planned to give Elizabeth something special and handmade. Everyone had a good idea, except me. But I knew I would think of something.

Stoneybrook Academy

"Four times eight is thirty-two, not thirty-four," Ricky Torres whispered loudly to Addie Sidney.

"Shh," I whispered to Ricky, just as loudly. "You know we are supposed to do our own work." Addie, Ricky, and I sit in the front row of Ms. Colman's second grade classroom. We were very busy with our math workbook exercises.

Ms. Colman looked up from her desk. She does not like people to talk in class without raising their hands. "Karen and Ricky, do you have a question?"

"Um, no," answered Ricky. He gave me a dirty look. I glared at him, too. (Actually, I was a little jealous that Ricky was helping Addie with her work when he was *my* pretend husband. We had gotten married at recess one day.)

Nancy Dawes raised her hand. "Ms. Colman, I am finished."

"Me, too," said Hannie Papadakis. Hannie and Nancy sit together in the back of the room. I sit in the front because I wear glasses.

"I am finished also," said Pamela Harding. (Pamela is my best enemy.)

Ms. Colman laughed. (She is a gigundoly wonderful teacher.) "All right, class. You may put away your workbooks for today. There is something I want to talk to you about." (Oh, goody. Ms. Colman always talks to us about interesting things.) "You know that tomorrow is Take Our Daughters

22

To Work Day," Ms. Colman continued. "How many of you will be going to work with your parents?"

I raised my hand. Then I looked around the room. Nancy, Hannie, Addie, and Pamela had raised their hands. So had Leslie Morris, Jannie Gilbert, Audrey Green, and Natalie Springer. So had the twins, Tammy and Terri Barkan. "Almost all the girls in this class are going to work," I announced. (I thought it would be all right to call out since my hand was already raised.)

Ms. Colman did not seem to mind. She nodded and said, "That's good. The rest of us are looking forward to hearing all about your day at work."

"What will they be doing at work all day?" Hank Reubens wanted to know.

"The girls will be learning about what their parents do," answered Ms. Colman. "They may even help them with some of their work."

"Yes," said Addie. "My mother said I

could help calm the animals who come in for their shots. She is an animal doctor." Addie moved her wheelchair closer to Hootie and Evelyn's cages and looked at them. (Hootie and Evelyn are our class guinea pigs.)

"Does your mother take care of guinea pigs?" asked Chris Lamar.

Addie nodded. "She takes care of all kinds of small animals, even snakes and lizards."

"Cool," said Chris.

"My mother is a writer," Pamela announced in a loud voice. "She is very busy. She told me I will have to help her answer the phone. It rings all the time."

"Big deal," I whispered.

"Karen, I can hear you," said Ricky. He was laughing.

Audrey told our class she was going to work in the kitchen of a famous French restaurant. "My father is the chef there."

"Will he let you bring us back some

food?" asked Bobby Gianelli. "Maybe some desserts?"

"Maybe," said Audrey, giggling.

I thought my classmates' parents had gigundoly cool jobs.

At Work

"Karen, are you ready?" Elizabeth called from downstairs.

"Almost," I called back. I checked in the mirror to see how I looked. I wore a blue blouse and a gray skirt, white tights, and black patent-leather shoes. I also carried my gray and red briefcase. (It was really my book bag.) I thought I looked very grown-up.

"Karen," Elizabeth called again.

"Coming!" I shouted. I checked inside my briefcase to make sure I had a notebook, my pencil case, and some crayons. I wanted to be prepared for my day at work.

First Elizabeth and I stopped at a diner in Stamford. (Stamford is the town where Elizabeth works.) Elizabeth ordered coffee. I ordered coffee, too, but I put lots of milk in mine. I made sure I stirred in a lot of sugar, too.

Elizabeth works in a big office building. A sign on the door said MAHLER AND GREYE, ADVERTISING. A big picture of a sun was on the sign. "The sun is our company's logo," said Elizabeth as she held open the door. "A logo is a symbol that helps people recognize us.

"Hello, Frank," said Elizabeth to the guard in the lobby. "This is Karen. She is coming to work with me today."

I stood up a little straighter and shook Frank's hand. I held my briefcase so Frank could see it.

Frank smiled and pushed a button to open the elevator door. (I think he thought I was an important visitor.) Elizabeth and I took the elevator to the twelfth floor. We en-

tered a large room with a huge window and lots of framed photographs hanging on the walls. (Elizabeth said those were advertisements.) I saw ads for soap, baseballs, and candles. I also saw a huge photo of silver and copper coins. Elizabeth said it was an ad for a department store.

"A department store?" I asked.

"Yes," said Elizabeth. "The coins show the money you will save by shopping there."

"Oh." (I guess that made sense.)

Elizabeth introduced me to more people. I met Ruth, the receptionist; Priscilla, a copywriter; and Gary, an art director. "Priscilla writes some of our ads, and Gary decides how they will look," Elizabeth explained.

I also saw other daughters with their mothers. (I was the only one carrying a briefcase.) Some of the daughters smiled at me. I smiled back.

A lot of the daughters were going to the art department. I loved the people in the art department. Most of them were wearing jeans and T-shirts. They sat at big tables or in front of computer screens. One man let me play with the squishy ball on his desk. A woman named Anna showed me her postcard collection and her Gumby doll. Elizabeth did not let me play with the Gumby doll too long. She wanted to get to her office.

Elizabeth did not have any squishy toys, dolls, or postcards on her desk. Instead she had a blotter, a pencil case, and a computer. She also had framed pictures of all the people in my big-house family.

Elizabeth put down her briefcase. I put my briefcase down, too. Elizabeth straightened her suit. I tucked in my blouse. Then Elizabeth showed me around the office some more. Here is what I liked the best:

1) The copy machine. (It was so huge, it took up almost a whole room.)

2) The fax machine. (It is a machine that can send and receive messages. When I was there, Elizabeth received a fax all the way from France.)

3) The candy machine. (It had my favorite kind of chocolate bar.)

4) The water cooler.

Finally, Elizabeth took me downstairs to the cafeteria. The cafeteria had sea-green walls and huge windows that looked out over the water. I could smell pizza, brownies, and fresh rolls baking in the oven.

"Would you like to eat lunch here?" asked Elizabeth.

"Sure," I answered. My day at work was getting better and better.

Phones, Faxes, and Photocopies

When we returned to Elizabeth's office, the phone was ringing, her assistant was coming in with her mail, and someone from the art department was waiting to see her. I sat in a corner of Elizabeth's office and watched her work.

First Elizabeth spoke on the phone. She talked about things like product lines and sales figures. (I did not know what those things meant.)

When Elizabeth's assistant came in again,

I tried to talk to her, but she looked busy, too. She brought Elizabeth letters to sign. Then she left to make copies.

"Oh, Karen, could you please make me a copy of this?" asked Elizabeth. She handed me a letter her assistant had forgotten to take. I nodded, and walked to the copy machine. I had to wait in line a long time. Then I had to ask someone how the copy machine worked. When I returned to Elizabeth's office, she was on the phone again. Boo and bullfrogs!

I was happy when Elizabeth said it was time to go to a meeting. Elizabeth picked up a binder, a notepad, and some pencils. I picked up my notepad and colored pencils. I followed Elizabeth down the hall to a big room. (Elizabeth said it was a conference room.) A lot of people in suits sat around a long table.

First a man stood up and passed around some charts. "These are the latest sales projections for the Steelhead account," he said.

I did not know what he was talking about. I tried to ask Elizabeth, but she put her finger to her lips. (I guess that meant I should be quiet during the meeting, at least until that person finished talking.) But guess what? That person talked and talked. It seemed like hours before he stopped. Then a woman in a blue dress held up something wrapped in pink and green paper. It looked like a very small bar of soap. And she started talking about something called "packaging."

I yawned — kind of loudly, I guess. Elizabeth looked at me and frowned. The woman in the blue dress kept talking. I stopped trying to understand what she was saying. Instead I took out my notepad. I decided to write a letter to Maxie. (Maxie is my pen pal in New York City.) This is what I wrote:

I AM SITTING IN A BORING, BORING MEETING IN AN AD AGENCY. ELIZABETH, TOOK ME TO WORK WITH HER. IT IS TAKE OUR

DAUGHTERS TO WORK DAY. ARE YOU AT
WORK WITH YOUR MOTHER OR FATHER?
PLEASE WRITE BACK.

LOVE,
KAREN

At the bottom of Maxie's letter I drew a picture of myself, and then I folded up the letter. (I did not want Elizabeth to see it.) Finally the meeting ended.

When Elizabeth asked me if I had any questions, I shook my head. I did not want to admit I had not been listening. Elizabeth was starting to tell me something about the meeting when Daddy and Kristy arrived.

I was very happy to see them. That meant we could have lunch together in the cafeteria. Then I could go to work with Daddy. I was sure his job was more exciting than Elizabeth's.

I was wrong. All Daddy did in his home office was talk on the phone, file letters, and send faxes. I tried to help. Once or twice, Daddy let me answer the phone. He even

36

showed me how to use the fax machine. But I had trouble staying awake. The insurance business was even less exciting than advertising. I was thrilled when Daddy said it was time to close up his office for the day. Daddy and Elizabeth sure had *boring* jobs.

Theaters, Restaurants, and Offices

The next day, I was very happy to be at school and not at work. I decided working in an office was not for me. It would be a lot more fun to be a famous actress or a rock star. That reminded me. I needed to ask Daddy if I could take singing lessons. I wanted to be prepared for my career on the stage.

"Karen," said Nancy. "Did you know Tammy and Terri spent all day at their uncle's theater?"

"They did?" (Hannie, Nancy, and I were sitting on desks in the back of our classroom, talking. We do that most mornings while we wait for Ms. Colman.)

"Yes, and they even got to watch a rehearsal."

"Cool," I said. (I was very impressed, but I was also a teensy, weensy bit jealous.)

"Good morning, class. Please take your seats now," said Ms. Colman when she entered the room. I hurried to my desk. Everyone quieted down.

"Ricky, would you please take attendance," said Ms. Colman. (Boo and bullfrogs. I like to be the one to take attendance. It is an important job.)

Ricky got busy looking around the room and marking Ms. Colman's attendance book. "Everyone is here," he announced.

"Good," said Ms. Colman, smiling at us. "Girls, the class would like to hear about your day at work yesterday. Who would like to speak first?"

Several girls raised their hands. I did not. First, Pamela Harding told us how busy she had been helping her mother. "I filed important papers and I answered the phone," said Pamela. "I even read some of her stories."

I loved it when Terri and Tammy talked about their day backstage at their uncle's theater. "We watched part of the rehearsal for *The Wizard of Oz*," said Tammy. "The actors were still learning their lines, so they read from scripts."

"We also helped paint scenery, and we threaded some needles for Mrs. Perkins. That's the person who sews the costumes," added Terri. "She was sewing a beautiful white and gold dress for Glinda."

"Who's Glinda?" asked Omar Harris.

"The good witch," answered Terri.

Audrey told the class about working in the kitchen in her father's restaurant. "You should see the pots and pans. They are huge!" Audrey spread out her arms while she talked. "The restaurant feeds hundreds of people every day, so they have to have a lot of food ready."

"Did you get to taste the food?" asked Bobby.

40

Audrey nodded. "I mostly tasted the desserts. I had a chocolate layer cake, a lemon mousse — that is like a lemon pudding — and some pies with apples, honey, and raisins in it."

My mouth started watering. Everyone's day at work sounded better than mine. Even the kids who went to offices had fun. Jannie Gilbert talked about her father's exciting job at the newspaper. "Everyone had to rush to get their stories in by the deadline. There were reporters typing at their keyboards until the last minute, and photographers coming in with their pictures, and phones ringing all the time."

"Karen, how was your day?" asked Ms. Colman when the others had finished. (I was hoping she would not call on me.)

"Uh, fine," I said. (I hoped it was okay to lie a little.) "In the morning, I went to work with Elizabeth. She's my stepmother." (I did not really have to explain. Most of the kids know about my two families.) "She works for an advertising agency. I, uh, went to a

41

big meeting with her. In the afternoon, Daddy took me to work with him. He works at home for an insurance company. He, um, let me answer the phone. And he taught me how to use the fax machine." I stopped talking. No one asked me any questions about my day. That was fine with me. It did sound pretty boring compared with the others.

Ms. Colman smiled at me. "Thank you, Karen," she said. "It sounds like you all learned a lot. We are going to continue learning about careers. I am planning a Career Week the week after next. I would like each of you to bring in one of your parents to talk to the class about his or her job."

I gulped.

"So, please start thinking about which of your parents you would like to invite to school," said Ms. Colman as the final bell rang.

"I do not want Daddy or Elizabeth to come to school," I muttered. But no one heard me. My classmates were packing up their books and rushing out the door.

9

A Big, Fat, Hairy Lie

A few days later Ms. Colman made another announcement. "Class," she began. "By the end of the day, I would like you to tell me which parent you plan to invite. I also need to know what your parents will be talking about."

Darn. I was hoping Ms. Colman had forgotten about Career Week. I still did not know what to do. I could not invite Elizabeth. Her job seemed way too boring. And Daddy's job had been even more boring than Elizabeth's. I sighed, and tried to concentrate on our lesson.

"Where is the Nile River?" asked Ms. Colman.

I did not raise my hand. (That is very unusual. I am usually the first one to raise my hand in class, especially when I know the answer.)

"In South America," answered Chris Lamar.

"No, it is not. It is in Africa," said Bobby Gianelli.

"Good, Bobby," said Ms. Colman.

Ms. Colman told us more about Africa. She showed us pictures of the African savannah. And she told us about some of the animals that live there — zebras, rhinoceroses, and lions. (I adore listening to Ms. Colman, but today I was having trouble paying attention. I was too worried about Career Week.)

At lunch I hardly ate anything. Nancy and Hannie were busy talking about inviting their fathers for Career Week. They did not notice that I was not eating or saying anything. That made me a little cross.

"Who are you inviting for Career Week?" Nancy finally asked me.

"I have not decided yet," I answered. Nancy gave me a funny look.

At recess I sat alone on a bench. "Karen, come play with us," said Hannie. She was jumping rope with Nancy, Natalie, and Audrey.

"I do not want to," I said. I wanted to think some more about who to invite.

I wished I could ask Mommy or Seth to come to school, instead of Daddy or Elizabeth. Seth works as a carpenter, and he makes beautiful things. Mommy sometimes helps him in his studio, but mostly she stays home and takes care of Andrew and me. Those jobs had to be more exciting than Daddy's or Elizabeth's. But I could not invite Mommy or Seth because this was a big-house month. And that would hurt Daddy's and Elizabeth's feelings.

My choice was between Daddy or Elizabeth. And I did not want either of them. Nothing I could do would make their jobs sound interesting. I would be the only one in the school with boring parents. This was *not fair*!

By the end of recess I was in an even worse mood. I stormed back to our classroom. I did not stop to talk to Hannie and Nancy.

"Girls and boys, have you decided which parent to invite?" asked Ms. Colman.

"Yes," answered my classmates.

When Ms. Colman called on me, I did not know what to say. Then I did something I knew was wrong. I lied. I told Ms. Colman that Daddy and Elizabeth could not come to school for Career Week. "They are both going to be out of town," I explained.

Ms. Colman smiled at me. "All right, Karen. We will not expect them then."

I felt like a rat.

A Picture, a Pillow,
and a Play

At dinner that night I was not very hungry. I still felt bad about lying to Ms. Colman.

"Karen," said Kristy after we finished eating. "We are having another meeting about Mom's birthday."

"Okay," I said. I was not in the mood to plan a party. But I forced myself. I plopped myself down on Kristy's beanbag chair.

"We have to talk about food and decorations," said Kristy.

"Cupcakes and candles," shouted Andrew.

"Shh," I said. "Elizabeth might hear you."

"Oops," whispered Andrew.

We talked about the food and decorations we would make. Kristy wrote everything down in her notebook. Here is what her list looked like:

Food

1. Lemonade — Karen will make.
2. Punch — Charlie will make.
3. Birthday cake — Kristy and Karen will bake and decorate with icing flowers.
4. Sandwiches — Sam, Charlie, David Michael, and Andrew will make.
5. Salads — Nannie will make? (Will have to ask her.)
6. Popcorn and potato chips — Kristy and Karen will buy.

Decorations

1. A giant card — from all of us. (We will draw pictures and write poems and funny notes in it.)
2. Balloons — use what we have in house.

3. Candles — use what we have in house.
4. Tablecloth and napkins — Kristy and Karen will buy.
5. Flowers — we will all pick big bunches from the garden.

"We could start working on the card right now," said Kristy. She rummaged behind her desk and pulled out a giant sheet of poster board, and some Magic Markers and colored pencils. I began drawing bouquets of daffodils in one corner of the light-blue board.

I was having a lot of fun, until Kristy started talking about Elizabeth's presents. That reminded me. I still had not thought of a good idea. I felt worse when I realized that everyone else had already started making their special gifts.

"Sam and I are working on the footstool," Charlie reported. He sat writing a funny poem to Elizabeth in one corner of the card.

"I am writing my play," said David

Michael. "It's about a magic sunflower called Marvin."

"What is magic about Marvin?" I asked.

"He is taller than all the other flowers in the garden. And he can talk," answered David Michael.

"What happens to Marvin?" I wanted to know.

"Um, I am still working on that."

"Could I be in your play?" I asked politely.

"Maybe," answered David Michael. "But so far Marvin is the only character."

I sighed. (I had been sighing a lot lately.)

Kristy pulled out the pillow she was making. It was shaped like a cat, and she was sewing on buttons for the nose and eyes. It looked gigundoly cool. Even Andrew had started working on his picture of a garden. Everyone except me was getting a present ready. I hoped I would think of something. I was feeling a little nervous.

Career Work

"Does anyone know what these are?" Natalie's father asked our class. He held up large sheets of blue paper with white lines drawn all over them.

"They look like plans for something," said Omar.

"Good," said Mr. Springer. He sounded very impressed with Omar. "They are indeed. They are the plans for a house. We call them blueprints." Mr. Springer is an architect. He gets to design all kinds of buildings. He showed us how to find the stairs, windows, and fireplaces on the plan. Then he told us the house had a secret passageway.

"Cool," said Chris.

"Could we come play in this house when it is finished?" asked Bobby. Everyone laughed.

It was the first day of Career Week. My classmates' parents were giving gigundoly good presentations. I still felt guilty about lying to Ms. Colman. But I was glad neither of my parents was coming to school. They would seem so boring next to the other parents.

I loved it when Terri and Tammy's uncle told us about his theater. He brought in real stage props — the things the actors hold in the play. He let us hold Glinda's magic wand and the broom that belonged to the Wicked Witch of the West. "There is someone backstage who only handles props. It is that person's job to find what we need for the show. He or she also takes care of all the props while the show is running."

Best of all, Mr. Barkan passed out some

scripts and let us act out some scenes from the play. I insisted on being Dorothy. (She is the star of the show.) Pamela and Nancy wanted to be Dorothy too. So we took turns. I think Mr. Barkan liked the way I read. He told me I had a voice that projects.

"What does that mean?" I asked.

"It means everyone in the theater will be able to hear you," answered Mr. Barkan.

I felt very proud.

Audrey's father came in wearing a big white chef's hat and an apron. He handed out some menus from his restaurant. I could not read most of the menu. Then I figured out why. A lot of it was written in French. The special was something called *canard à l'orange*. Mr. Green told us that was duck with orange sauce.

"People really eat ducks?" asked Ian.

Mr. Green nodded. "Yes, and snails, rabbits, calves' legs, frogs' legs, and sheep's intestines."

I gulped. Natalie Springer turned pale. Ricky looked like he might be sick. Luckily

Mr. Green did not bring in samples of those foods. Instead he gave us some tiny cakes that tasted like raspberry and chocolate. He said they were called petit fours. He also said they were his specialty. My class loved them. "It is the dessert I am well known for," he explained.

"Do all chefs have a specialty?" asked Addie.

"Yes," answered Mr. Green. "A lot of chefs invent special dishes and name them after themselves."

"Cool," said Bobby. "I want to invent my own ice-cream sundae and call it the Gianelli Special."

Mr. Green laughed.

"Weren't those presentations fun?" asked Hannie. Hannie, Nancy, and I were walking to the lunchroom. (None of us was too hungry, though. Not after all those petit fours.)

"Gigundoly fun," I replied.

"Too bad your parents cannot come in this week," said Hannie.

"Um, yeah," I answered. (I felt bad not telling Hannie and Nancy the truth. But I felt so embarrassed about lying to Ms. Colman that I did not want my best friends to know what I had done.)

12

Trouble

It was the last day of Career Week. Addie's mother was telling us about being an animal doctor. "In one day, you might check a dog for mites, X-ray a cat, and perform surgery on a rabbit," she said.

"What are mites?" I asked.

"Like fleas, only smaller," answered Dr. Sidney.

Yuck. I do not like fleas. But I did think it would be cool to meet all kinds of rabbits, cats, and dogs and help them feel better.

Maybe I could be an animal doctor. (After my career onstage, that is.)

"How do you know an animal is sick when it can't talk to you?" asked Hannie.

"Good question," answered Dr. Sidney. "You have to pay attention to what its owner tells you. And you have to examine your patient carefully — look into its eyes, take its temperature, listen to its heart and lungs."

I wanted to ask Dr. Sidney a million more questions. For instance, is it bad for Boo-Boo to be so fat? But Ms. Colman said Hannie's question had to be the last one. School was over for the day. That meant Career Week was over too. (Whew.)

"Karen," said Elizabeth at dinner that night. "I ran into Natalie Springer's father at lunchtime. He asked me if I was going to talk to your class for Career Week."

I gulped. Then I took a long drink of water. (My stomach was feeling a little funny.)

"When is Career Week?" asked Elizabeth.

"Um, um . . . I think it is, uh, next week sometime."

Just then the phone rang. (Whew.) Daddy got up to answer it. I tried to finish eating. We were having fried chicken and mashed potatoes. That is one of my favorite meals.

When Daddy came back to the table, he looked angry. Very angry. "Karen, that was Ms. Colman," he said. "She was calling to ask Nannie to help out with a bake sale. She was surprised to find me at home. She thought Elizabeth and I were out of town."

"Oh," I said, sighing. I stared at my plate. My food did not look so good anymore. Everyone else in my big-house family had stopped eating and talking. They were all looking at me. The room was very still.

"Karen," Daddy continued. (He says my name a lot when he is mad.) "Career Week was this past week. Ms. Colman told me everything."

Uh-oh. I knew I was in *big* trouble.

A Long Talk

After dinner, Daddy and Elizabeth took me to my room. They wanted to talk.

"Karen," Daddy began after we had sat down on my bed. "Why did you lie to Ms. Colman — and to us — about Career Week?"

"Um, um," I said. I picked up Moosie and looked at him. He stared back at me with his glass eyes. He did not know what to say either.

"Karen, I am waiting for an answer," said Daddy. He was still very mad.

61

"Um, well, you see," I finally said, "I, uh, did not want Elizabeth and you to come talk to my class because . . ." I sighed, and leaned back against my lacy white pillows. I felt like crying.

"Because why?" asked Elizabeth softly. She did not look as mad as Daddy.

"Because, um, you both have sort of unexciting jobs. I mean, unexciting compared to the other parents in my class. You see, Addie's mother is an animal doctor, and Audrey's father is a chef. He brought in all this great food for us to eat."

Daddy and Elizabeth did not look impressed. Instead they seemed hurt.

"Karen, let me understand this. You did not want your father or me to come to your class because you thought we would be too boring," said Elizabeth.

"Um, yeah."

Elizabeth sighed. Daddy shook his head.

"Even if that were true, it would not be a good reason to lie to Ms. Colman and to us," said Daddy. "You had a responsibility to your class and teacher. And you let them down."

I nodded. Then I started crying. I could not help it. "I did feel bad about lying," I said.

"Besides," Daddy continued, "how do you think Elizabeth and I feel? How would you feel if we decided your school was boring? So boring we would not even listen when you told us about it?"

I gulped. I had not thought about it that way. "I am sorry I hurt your feelings," I said. I felt terrible. "And I'm sorry I lied."

Daddy and Elizabeth looked at each other. "I accept your apology, Karen," said Elizabeth.

Daddy nodded. "But what you did was very serious, Karen. We have to punish you." (I had known that was coming.)

"How?" I asked.

"Next week you will come straight home after school every day and do your chores and homework," answered Daddy. "You will not be allowed to play with your friends, and they cannot come visit you. Is that understood?"

I nodded. (My punishment was bad, but not as bad as I had thought it would be.)

"And," Daddy continued, "you will apologize to Ms. Colman in person on Monday morning."

I promised Daddy that I would.

Heads or Tails

On Monday I went to school early. I was hoping Ms. Colman would be there early, too. But she was not. Instead I sat in the back of the room and talked to Hannie and Nancy. I told them all about lying to Ms. Colman and about my punishment.

"Wow," said Hannie. "I did not know your parents were in town. Why didn't you tell us?" (We had been playing at Hannie's house all week. Hannie and Nancy never knew if Daddy or Elizabeth was home or not.)

I looked down at the floor. "I guess I was embarrassed about lying to Ms. Colman," I said. "I did not want to lie to you, too." I pushed my glasses up on my nose.

Hannie and Nancy looked at me. They seemed to understand. Best friends usually understand each other. Sometimes I feel that they can read my mind, and I can read theirs.

"Ooh, there is Ms. Colman," said Nancy.

I knew what she was thinking. I waved good-bye to my friends and hurried to my teacher's desk. "Ms. Colman," I blurted out before she had time to sit down. "I have something to tell you."

Ms. Colman looked up. "Yes, Karen?"

"I am sorry I lied about my parents being out of town for Career Week."

"I am sorry you did, too, Karen. That was not like you."

"I am being punished for it." I told Ms. Colman about my punishment.

"Karen, I accept your apology," said Ms. Colman. "But you must now choose one of

your parents to come talk to our class about his or her career."

"I do?" I said. (This was news.)

"Yes," Ms. Colman said firmly. "All the other students did. I expect your decision by tomorrow."

Darn.

That afternoon I hurried home. I started studying for my spelling test. But mostly I thought and thought about Daddy and Elizabeth. And about their jobs. If Elizabeth came to my class, she could tell about talking on the phone and going to long, boring meetings. If Daddy came to my class, he could talk about sending faxes. I groaned. I still did not want either one. And now I was worrying about something else. Would Daddy feel bad if I chose Elizabeth instead of him? Or the other way around?

"What should I do?" I asked Shannon. He scampered into my room, wagging his tail. "Should I pick Daddy or Elizabeth?"

Shannon kept wagging his tail. I finally decided (without Shannon's help) that I would rather have Elizabeth. Her job was a little more exciting than Daddy's. And she could bring in pictures of some cool ads. But I did not want to hurt Daddy's feelings. So I thought of a great way to ask them.

After dinner I asked Daddy and Elizabeth to flip a coin. "Whoever gets heads first comes to my class," I said.

Daddy flipped the coin first. "Tails," he announced.

Elizabeth flicked the coin high in the air with her thumb. "Heads," she yelled when it came down.

Whew, I said to myself.

15

Marvin and Sassy Sally

"Who wants to be in my play?" asked David Michael.

"I do, I do," I said. "What parts are there?"

"Well, Marvin the sunflower," said David Michael. "And the gardener who takes care of Marvin. And a hen and a rabbit."

"I want to be Marvin," I said.

"You cannot play Marvin. That is my part," said David Michael. "I have already learned most of my lines."

Boo and bullfrogs. I wanted to be the star

of the show. "Well," I said, "I will need to read your play before I can decide what part I want."

"Okay." David Michael handed me a loose-leaf notebook. His handwriting was very hard to read.

We were all sitting in Kristy's room again. And guess what we were talking about? Elizabeth's party. Kristy reminded me that we needed to go shopping.

Yikes. The party was only one week away, and I still had not thought of a good present for Elizabeth. Everyone else's presents were ready. David Michael had finished writing his play. Andrew was putting the final touches on his picture of the garden. He was drawing red roses, blue lilacs, and some yellow things he said were daffodils. (They did not look like roses, lilacs, and daffodils to me. But I was sure Elizabeth would like his picture anyway.)

"Sam said he would help me frame it," said Andrew proudly as he made more yellow smudges on the paper.

Sam and Charlie had just about finished their footstool. Sam said it looked beautiful. "All we have to do is stain it," said Charlie.

Kristy showed everyone her cat pillow. She had sewn on buttons for the nose and eyes. She had made a tail. And she had put a lot of stuffing in the pillow so it looked very comfortable.

"That is a fat cat like Boo-Boo," said Andrew. We all laughed.

"Where is your present, Karen?" asked Kristy.

"Um, I do not have one yet," I said. (I was feeling more and more nervous. I hoped I would think of something soon.)

While the others worked on Elizabeth's giant card, I tried to read David Michael's play. Marvin the sunflower was the tallest flower in the garden. He was the only flower who could see over the garden wall. One night he overheard the gardener talking to himself. The gardener said, "I would like to wring my hen's neck."

"Ugh!" I tapped David Michael on the shoulder. "Does the gardener really wring the hen's neck? That is so gross. And mean."

"Keep reading, Karen."

Marvin liked the hen. Her name was Sassy Sally.

"Sassy Sally!" I cried. "That is so funny."

My brothers looked up. "Karen," said Charlie. "Try to control yourself." But he was laughing, too.

"What does sassy mean?" Andrew wanted to know.

"It means the hen talks back to people," explained Sam. "She does not care what other people think of her."

I kept reading. My brothers and Kristy worked on the card. The room grew very quiet.

"So what happens at the end of the play?" asked Sam after I had been reading quietly for awhile.

"Marvin tells his friend the rabbit to warn Sassy Sally," I said, giggling. "The rabbit does. And that night the hen struts away from the garden. The rabbit hops after her, and they take Marvin with them."

"And everywhere they go, everyone is really impressed with Marvin because he can talk," said David Michael.

(I decided this would not be a good time to tell David Michael that sunflowers die if they are cut. Also, flowers cannot talk.)

"That is a good story," said Andrew. "Can I be the rabbit?"

"Sure," said David Michael.

"Please, please let me play Sassy Sally," I pleaded.

"All right, Karen," said David Michael. "That is a good part for you."

Sam said he would be the gardener. We started rehearsing that night. But I could not concentrate. I was too worried about Elizabeth's present. I was the only one without a gift. And I was worried about Elizabeth boring my class the next day. (Sigh.) I had a lot of problems.

Wacky Cracky Bubble Gum

I woke up feeling a little sick to my stomach. Then I remembered why. Elizabeth was going to talk to my class. In a few hours my whole class would know that all Elizabeth does at work is talk on the phone and go to boring meetings. She could say that in ten seconds. And she would not have a fun demonstration or anything. Not like the other parents.

I pulled the covers over my face.

"Karen!" Nannie called. "You will be late for school."

I dragged myself out of bed and dressed slowly. I was so late that Nannie gave me a muffin to eat on the way to school.

As I was walking to my bus, Elizabeth stopped me. "Oh, Karen," she said, "I will be coming to your class for the entire afternoon."

"Really?" I did not have time to ask Elizabeth why she was going to stay for so long. My bus was pulling up to the curb. I ran to catch it.

I worried all morning about Elizabeth's demonstration. What could she have to say that would take an entire afternoon?

I came in from recess and found Elizabeth in our classroom, talking to Ms. Colman.

"Class," Ms. Colman began after we had sat down, "please welcome Elizabeth Thomas Brewer. She is going to speak to us about her career in advertising."

The kids in my class clapped. I forced myself to join in.

"Good afternoon. I am very glad to be here," said Elizabeth. Then she explained that her job is to figure out how to advertise new products. I sat up in my chair. Elizabeth made her job sound very interesting. My stomach started feeling normal again. "My company's newest client is Wacky Cracky Bubble Gum — bubble gum that crackles."

"Cool!" shouted Bobby.

I felt my eyes grow rounder. Elizabeth talked about the gum and how it is wrapped in bright colors — lime green and hot pink — to appeal to kids. (I had the feeling I should have paid more attention in Elizabeth's meeting. Those little packages I thought were soap may have been bubble gum.)

"My job is to produce a television commercial for this gum," said Elizabeth. "And" — Elizabeth paused and looked at us — "all of you, including Ms. Colman, are going to be in the commercial, this very afternoon."

"We are?" asked Pamela. She looked thrilled. So did the other kids.

Just then the door to our classroom

opened. In walked four people. One pushed a big camera, which sat on a wide platform with wheels. Another carried cables and a huge microphone. Two others pushed some lights. "This is the film crew," announced Elizabeth. My mouth dropped open.

"To make a commercial, you need a camera to film the scene, lights to spotlight the actors, and a microphone to pick up the sound," explained Elizabeth. "The scene we will shoot will be of all of you — and Ms. Colman — enjoying Wacky Cracky Bubble Gum. The director will explain everything you need to do. So please listen to her." Elizabeth nodded in the direction of a woman who was helping to set up the lights. Then Elizabeth passed around samples of the gum.

I could not believe this. Me — and my class — on TV. This was way too cool.

Lights, Camera, Action!

The camera crew was very busy. Two people set up the lights. Another man attached the microphone to the end of a long metal pole. "That microphone is called a boom," explained Elizabeth. "It will pick up the crackling noises the gum makes. Now, do not forget to blow bubbles during the filming."

"No problem," said Bobby. He was having a contest with Pamela to see who could blow the biggest bubbles. Then Omar and Jannie tried to make the loudest crackling sounds.

I watched the film crew and chewed the gum. It tasted like bananas and strawberries. Ricky said it reminded him of a banana smoothie. "The kind you can get at King Kone's," he added. (King Kone's is a big ice-cream store in Stoneybrook.) That is a real compliment, because Ricky loves everything at King Kone's.

Soon the woman called the director started rearranging our desks and chairs. She put them in neat rows. She also made Ian, Natalie, and Ricky comb their hair. And she asked Natalie to straighten her sweater and pull up her knee socks. "Don't you want to look neat for the camera?" she teased. (Natalie hardly ever looks neat.) The director made me button the collar of my shirt. And she asked some other kids to tuck in their shirts and blouses. "You have to look your best," she told us.

Then the director peered through the camera. Some of the kids in my class froze. But not me. I love being on film. I smiled and fluttered my eyelashes. I wished I had my sunglasses. Then I would really have looked like a star.

"Don't worry. We are not rolling yet," said the director.

"Oh." (I was disappointed.)

"What does she mean?" whispered Ricky.

"She means we are not being filmed yet," I whispered back.

"I am adjusting the camera," the director explained. "I will let you know when we're ready to begin." The director told us it was important to act natural. "Try to forget you're being filmed," she said. "Just pretend you're sitting with your friends enjoying Wacky Cracky Bubble Gum. Blow bubbles. Make crackling noises. Have fun. But make sure you stay seated at your desks. I do not want anyone running around the room or getting too rowdy."

I thought the director was a great person.

Soon the director nodded at the man holding the boom. Then she turned back to

us. "When you hear me say 'action,' that means the filming has begun," the director explained.

First one of the men held up a big piece of slate that looked like a blackboard. (Elizabeth said it was a clapboard.) "Scene one, take one," he said. Then he clapped two pieces of wood on the board together.

"Roll camera," said the director. "Action!"

My class chewed like crazy. We blew huge bubbles. We popped them. We crackled. (Or at least the gum did.) Once a giant bubble exploded in Bobby's face. Another time Natalie spit out her gum by mistake.

The director did five takes. "That means I am shooting this scene five times," she explained. She also told us our classroom scene was only part of the commercial. "The finished commercial will have lots of kids in different places enjoying the gum," she said.

My class did not care. We were having too much fun. Best of all, every single one of us was going to be in a TV commercial. Even Ms. Colman. I was thrilled.

A Talk with Elizabeth

"When will we see ourselves on TV?" asked Bobby as the film crew was packing up their equipment.

"The commercial should be on the air in about one month," said Elizabeth. "The client has to approve it first."

A month seemed like a long time. But I was not going to complain. I was in a wonderful mood. Elizabeth's presentation had been the best of all. Everyone in my class thought so, too.

"Elizabeth, I loved your talk," I said in the

car after school. (Elizabeth was not going back to work that afternoon. Instead she was coming home with me.) "I did not know you got to make TV commercials."

Elizabeth looked surprised. "Karen, you spent a whole morning at work with me. We were talking about the commercial in the meeting you went to. Remember?"

"Oh," I said. Elizabeth looked at me sideways. "Um, I was not really paying attention during the meeting," I confessed. "I got kind of bored when that man talked and talked about stuff I did not understand. So I stopped listening."

Elizabeth nodded. "I think I am beginning to understand what happened," she said.

I felt embarrassed.

"I am not mad, Karen. That was a busy morning, and I did not have time to explain a lot of things about my job to you. But when I asked if you had any questions, you could have told me you did not understand what was happening in the meeting. I would not have bitten your head off," said Elizabeth, smiling.

I giggled. "Well, yes. I guess so."

Elizabeth talked to me about honesty and about paying attention. "You know, Karen, professional people pay attention to what is happening around them. They notice things, and that is how they learn more about a business."

That made sense. I thought about what I had paid attention to in the advertising agency — the candy machine, the water cooler, the copy machine, Elizabeth's office. How everything in Elizabeth's office was so neat. She had a blotter, a pencil case, and photos in beautiful red leather frames of everyone in my big-house family. Hmm . . . the photos. Suddenly I got a gigundoly brilliant idea for Elizabeth's present. But of course I could not tell her about it.

"This has been a perfect day," I said, snuggling into my seat.

Elizabeth smiled at me and turned into our driveway. "I am glad you thought so, Karen."

19

A Special Present
for Elizabeth

As soon as Elizabeth parked the car, I raced inside the house.

"Guess what!" I shouted to Nannie and Emily Michelle. They were in the kitchen having an afternoon snack. (Actually, only Emily was. Nannie was pouring her some juice.)

"What?" asked Nannie.

"My class and I and even my teacher are going to be on television. We are all in a commercial Elizabeth is making," I shrieked.

"Oh, Karen, that is wonderful," said Nannie.

I grabbed Nannie's hands and we danced around the kitchen. Elizabeth came in and laughed.

"Would you like a snack, Karen?" asked Nannie.

"No, thank you," I said. (I did not have time to eat. I was too excited about making Elizabeth's present.)

I went upstairs to my room. I pulled out my stack of magazines from under my bed. I found paste, scissors, and paper in my desk. Then I looked around for pictures of everyone in my big-house family. In the study I saw a bunch of photos that had not been put into albums. (They were all doubles.) I also found some extra school pictures. I took all the pictures back to my room without anyone seeing me.

Finally I sat down to make Elizabeth a very special present — a collage of everyone in my big-house family. In the car I had realized that Elizabeth did not have a picture of my entire big-house family together. Her office needed one.

I was very busy. I cut faces from the pictures. I cut people's bodies from the magazines. I glued Sam's face to the body of a football player. I put Emily Michelle's face on the body of a little girl dressing up in her mother's clothes. I pasted my face to the body of a ballerina. Kristy was hard. I could not decide what body to paste her head on. Then I found a girl dressed in a softball uniform. Perfect. I put Kristy's face on the softball player. (Kristy is the coach of a softball team.)

I had a lot of fun arranging everyone on the big piece of paper. I put Kristy next to me. I had Daddy throwing Emily Michelle high in the air. Finally, when I was happy with the way the collage looked, I carefully glued all ten people in my big-house family onto the paper.

The next afternoon I found some fancy wrapping paper and cardboard. Then I sat down and made a picture frame for my collage. Here is what I did:

1) I cut the cardboard into a big rectangle-shaped frame that would fit around my collage.

2) I pasted the fancy paper onto the cardboard. (None of the cardboard showed afterward.)

3) I glued the picture frame onto the collage.

I had enough fancy paper left over to wrap the present. Then I tied it with a big lavender bow. There. A very special present for Elizabeth.

Party Time

When I woke up on Saturday, I blinked. The sun shone through my window. I heard robins and sparrows chirping. It was a beautiful day for Elizabeth's party. I bounded out of bed.

"Karen, have some breakfast," said Nannie. Andrew, David Michael, Daddy, Elizabeth, and Emily Michelle sat eating French toast.

"Where are Kristy, Sam, and Charlie?" I asked.

"Oh, they have been up for hours," said

Nannie, winking. "They are outside in the backyard."

I found Kristy, Sam, and Charlie setting up tables in the backyard.

"Have you really been up for hours?" I asked.

"Of course," teased Sam. "Who do you think does all the work around here?"

Kristy laughed. "Sam," she said. "We have not been up that long. We are just starting to set up. Get dressed and have some breakfast, Karen. Then come help us. We have a lot to do. Andrew and David Michael are going to keep Mom busy so she does not come out here."

We really did have a lot to do to get ready. These are the things we did:

1) Set the tables with white tablecloths, plastic knives, forks, and spoons, and paper cups, plates, and napkins. (The paper plates and cups were blue, the napkins yellow.) We set up three tables — one to hold the food, and the other two to eat on.

2) Mixed punch and lemonade.

3) Blew up balloons.

4) Put chairs around the tables.

5) Gathered bunches of flowers for the tables.

6) Set the food and presents out on the big table.

We were all ready by lunchtime. I ran to find David Michael, Andrew, Daddy, and Elizabeth and I brought them out to the backyard.

"Surprise!" everyone yelled. Except Shannon and Boo-Boo, of course. But they wagged their tails. Kristy had tied yellow bows around their necks.

"Oh, my," said Elizabeth. "Everything is so pretty." She looked like she was trying very hard not to cry. Daddy gave Elizabeth a hug. The rest of us hugged her, too.

Then we ate. I ate three little sandwiches: tuna, egg salad, and ham. Then I ate some potato chips and fruit. Then more potato chips. Then lots of lemonade.

"Everything tastes wonderful," said Elizabeth.

"Time for dessert," announced Nannie, nodding at Kristy and me. Soon Kristy came outside carrying the big chocolate birthday cake. I walked beside her. The cake had three yellow candles on it. ("Grown-ups do not like to be reminded of their age," Kristy had told me when we were making the cake.)

Elizabeth blew out the candles in one breath. Andrew and David Michael put a lot of vanilla ice cream on their cake. I did not. I thought it tasted gigundoly good just the way it was.

Then came the best part of the party. Elizabeth opened her presents. She loved her giant card and spent a lot of time reading all the funny notes we wrote in it. I hopped on one foot. Then the other. I could not wait for Elizabeth to open my present.

"Oh, Karen, what a wonderful idea," Elizabeth said when she unwrapped my gift. She held it up so everyone could see it.

"How come I am wearing a cat costume?" asked Andrew.

"I was being creative," I answered.

"Where did you find the bowling ball for me?" asked Nannie.

"In a magazine," I said. Everyone loved my collage. They spent a long time looking at it.

"And now for the play," said David Michael.

"A play?" asked Elizabeth.

"Yes, I wrote it myself," said David Michael.

I ran inside to change into my Sassy Sally costume. I wore white tights, a white T-shirt, and a beak. Kristy pinned some feathers in my hair.

David Michael put on his Marvin outfit. He wore a chain of daffodils around his neck.

"I am a sunflower named Marvin," said David Michael. "I am the tallest flower in the garden."

Elizabeth chuckled.

Everyone laughed a lot during the play. They especially liked the part when Marvin saved Sassy Sally's life. At the end, I strutted away like a hen.

When the play was over, everyone stood up and cheered. I felt very proud.

"Three cheers for David Michael," called Daddy.

"Three cheers for Elizabeth," I cried.

"Hooray! Hooray! Hooray!" we cheered.

About the Author

ANN M. MARTIN lives in New York City and loves animals, especially cats. She has two cats of her own, Gussie and Woody.

Other books by Ann M. Martin that you might enjoy are *Stage Fright; Me and Katie (the Pest);* and the books in *The Baby-sitters Club* series.

Ann likes ice cream and *I Love Lucy.* And she has her own little sister, whose name is Jane.

Little Sister

Don't miss #85

KAREN'S TREASURE

"Wow!" said Andrew. "There *is* something in here!"

"Let *me* see." I grabbed the magnifying glass. Sure enough, there was something in the hole. It looked like a piece of paper. It was rolled up like a scroll.

"Can you pull it out?" I asked. Andrew's fingers were smaller than mine. He squeezed them in and grabbed the edge of the paper.

When Andrew had the paper halfway out, he looked up and grinned at me.

"Good work," I told him. "I will take over now."

I worked the paper out the rest of the way. It was old and yellow. I unrolled it very carefully. You will never guess what it was. It was a treasure map!

LITTLE 🍎 APPLE™

BABY-SITTERS™
Little Sister

by Ann M. Martin,
author of The Baby-sitters Club ®

More Titles... ➡

❑	MQ48230-0	#55	Karen's Magician	$2.95
❑	MQ48302-1	#56	Karen's Ice Skates	$2.95
❑	MQ48303-X	#57	Karen's School Mystery	$2.95
❑	MQ48304-8	#58	Karen's Ski Trip	$2.95
❑	MQ48231-9	#59	Karen's Leprechaun	$2.95
❑	MQ48305-6	#60	Karen's Pony	$2.95
❑	MQ48306-4	#61	Karen's Tattletale	$2.95
❑	MQ48307-2	#62	Karen's New Bike	$2.95
❑	MQ25996-2	#63	Karen's Movie	$2.95
❑	MQ25997-0	#64	Karen's Lemonade Stand	$2.95
❑	MQ25998-9	#65	Karen's Toys	$2.95
❑	MQ26279-3	#66	Karen's Monsters	$2.95
❑	MQ26024-3	#67	Karen's Turkey Day	$2.95
❑	MQ26025-1	#68	Karen's Angel	$2.95
❑	MQ26193-2	#69	Karen's Big Sister	$2.95
❑	MQ26280-7	#70	Karen's Grandad	$2.95
❑	MQ26194-0	#71	Karen's Island Adventure	$2.95
❑	MQ26195-9	#72	Karen's New Puppy	$2.95
❑	MQ26301-3	#73	Karen's Dinosaur	$2.95
❑	MQ26214-9	#74	Karen's Softball Mystery	$2.95
❑	MQ69183-X	#75	Karen's County Fair	$2.95
❑	MQ69184-8	#76	Karen's Magic Garden	$2.95
❑	MQ69185-6	#77	Karen's School Surprise	$2.99
❑	MQ69186-4	#78	Karen's Half Birthday	$2.99
❑	MQ69187-2	#79	Karen's Big Fight	$2.99
❑	MQ69188-0	#80	Karen's Christmas Tree	$2.99
❑	MQ69189-9	#81	Karen's Accident	$2.99
❑	MQ69190-2	#82	Karen's Secret Valentine	$3.50
❑	MQ69191-0	#83	Karen's Bunny	$3.50
❑	MQ69192-9	#84	Karen's Big Job	$3.50
❑	MQ69193-7	#85	Karen's Treasure	$3.50
❑	MQ55407-7		BSLS Jump Rope Pack	$5.99
❑	MQ73914-X		BSLS Playground Games Pack	$5.99
❑	MQ89735-7		BSLS Photo Scrapbook Book and Camera Pack	$9.99
❑	MQ47677-7		BSLS School Scrapbook	$2.95
❑	MQ43647-3		Karen's Wish Super Special #1	$3.25
❑	MQ44834-X		Karen's Plane Trip Super Special #2	$3.25
❑	MQ44827-7		Karen's Mystery Super Special #3	$3.25
❑	MQ45644-X		Karen, Hannie, and Nancy	
			The Three Musketeers Super Special #4	$2.95
❑	MQ45649-0		Karen's Baby Super Special #5	$3.50
❑	MQ46911-8		Karen's Campout Super Special #6	$3.25

Available wherever you buy books, or use this order form.

Scholastic Inc., P.O. Box 7502, 2931 E. McCarty Street, Jefferson City, MO 65102

Please send me the books I have checked above. I am enclosing $ _____
(please add $2.00 to cover shipping and handling). Send check or money order – no
cash or C.O.Ds please.

Name _____ Birthdate _____

Address _____

City _____ State/Zip _____

Please allow four to six weeks for delivery. Offer good in U.S.A. only. Sorry, mail orders are not
available to residents to Canada. Prices subject to change.   BLS1096

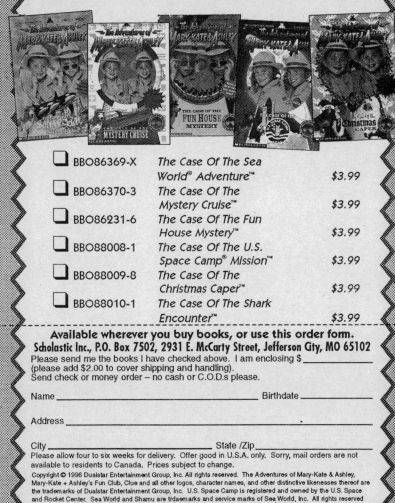